HENRY and MUDGE
GET THE
Cold Shivers

The Seventh Book of Their Adventures

Story by Cynthia Rylant

Pictures by Suçie Stevenson

SCHOLASTIC INC.

New York Toronto London Auckland Sydney
Mexico City New Delhi Hong Kong Buenos Aires

To Jennifer and Karen Stone—CR

For James Walker Stevenson—SS

No part of this publication may be reproduced in whole or in part,
or stored in a retrieval system, or transmitted in any form or by any means,
electronic, mechanical, photocopying, recording, or otherwise, without
written permission of the publisher. For information regarding permission,
write to Simon & Schuster Books for Young Readers, Simon & Schuster
Children's Publishing Division, 1230 Avenue of the Americas,
New York, NY 10020.

ISBN 0-590-98235-4

Text copyright © 1989 by Cynthia Rylant.
Illustrations copyright © 1989 by Suçie Stevenson.
All rights reserved.
Published by Scholastic Inc., 557 Broadway, New York, NY 10012,
by arrangement with Simon & Schuster Books for Young Readers,
Simon & Schuster Children's Publishing Division.
SCHOLASTIC and associated logos are trademarks and/or
registered trademarks of Scholastic Inc.

12 11 10   7 8/0

Printed in the U.S.A.   23

First Scholastic printing, September 2003

The text of this book is set in 18-point Goudy Old Style.
The illustrations are pen-and-ink and watercolor,
reproduced in full color.
Cover redesigned by Christopher A. Motil.

Contents

The Sick Day

Henry's big dog Mudge
loved Henry's sick days.

When Henry had a sore throat
or a fever
or a bad cough,
he stayed home
from school in bed.

In the morning
Henry's mother brought him
orange Popsicles,
comic books,
and crackers.

Mudge got the crackers.

In the evening
Henry's father brought him
grape Popsicles,
comic books,
and crackers.

Mudge got the crackers again.

Mudge *loved* sick days.

But even though he loved
Henry's sick days,
no one ever thought
that *Mudge* would get sick.

No one ever thought
that Mudge could catch germs.
But he could,
and one day he caught
a lot of them.

When Henry woke up
and jumped out of bed,
Mudge didn't move.
He didn't get up.
He didn't lick Henry's face.

He didn't even shake Henry's hand,
and he always shook Henry's hand
in the morning.

He just looked at Henry
and wagged his tail a little.

Henry and Henry's mother
looked at Mudge and worried.

"Something's wrong," said Henry.

His mother nodded her head.

"Mudge must be sick," said Henry.

His mother nodded her head again.

"Mudge," said Henry, "are you
just wanting some crackers?"

But Mudge didn't want crackers.

Mudge was sick—
and he didn't even *read*
comic books.

The Vet

Henry and Henry's mother
tried to put Mudge in the car
to go to the doctor.
But Mudge was tired.
He didn't want to go.

"Hop in, Mudge,"
said Henry.
Mudge sat down on Henry's foot.

"Hop, Mudge,"
Henry said again.
Mudge yawned and drooled
on Henry's hand.

"Bath time, Mudge," Henry said,
and Mudge hopped right in the car.
They drove to the vet.

Mudge knew the vet—
and he didn't want to see her.
She made him nervous.

When they walked
into her waiting room,
Mudge started to shiver
and shed.

He did this every time
he went to the vet.
He shivered and shed.

He always left a bunch
of dog hair
on her floor.

When it was his turn
to see the vet,
Henry and Henry's mother
had to pull him
like a horse
into the room.

"Hi, Mudge," said the vet.

Mudge shivered.

"Bad day, Mudge?" said the vet.

Mudge shed.

"He's losing all his hair,"
said Henry.
"I know," said the vet.
"I'd better hurry,
or he may be bald
before you can get him home."
Henry's mother laughed.

But Henry couldn't laugh.

He was too worried.

He was too scared.

The vet looked at Mudge's wet eyes.

She listened to
Mudge's shivering chest.

She felt Mudge's
shedding stomach.

Then she rubbed
Mudge's big head.

"I need to check a few things,"

she told Henry.

"Can you wait outside?"

Henry wanted to say no.

Henry wanted to say *no way*.

But Henry said, "All right."

He went back to the
waiting room with his mother.
He sat and wondered if Mudge
knew how to say "ah."

He wondered if Mudge
would be okay.

A Big Kiss

"Your dog has a cold,"
the vet told Henry.
"A *cold?*" said Henry.
"I think so," said the vet.

"He has a fever,
his throat is red,
he's very tired,
and he keeps asking me
for some comic books."
This time Henry could laugh.

"You have to let
him rest," said the vet.
Henry nodded.

"And give him his medicine."
Henry nodded again.

"And don't kiss him
until he's better,"
the vet said.
Henry frowned.
"Aw," he said.

When Henry and Henry's mother
and Mudge got home,
Henry fixed a sickbed
for Mudge in the living room.

It had Henry's old blanket in it
and five of Henry's dirty socks
and Henry's baseball mitt
and Henry's pillow
and a stuffed moose.

The next morning
Henry brought Mudge
some ice cubes,
a rubber hamburger,
and crackers.

Henry got the crackers.

In the evening
Henry brought Mudge
some ice cubes,
a rubber hot dog,
and crackers.

Henry got the crackers again.

But the next day,

Mudge ate *all* of the crackers.

His sick days were over.

And Henry gave him a great big kiss.